Shout, Show and Tell!

Written by

Kate Agnew

Illustrated by

Lydia Monks

Green Bananas

Crabtree Publishing Company
www.crabtreebooks.com

PMB 16A, 350 Fifth Avenue,
Suite 3308,
New York, NY 10118

616 Welland Avenue,
St. Catharines, Ontario
Canada, L2M 5V6

Agnew, Kate.
Shout, show, and tell / written by Kate Agnew ; illustrated by Lydia Monks.
p. cm. -- (Green bananas)
Summary: Three brief stories, all set in school, about Daisy's wobbly tooth, noisy Sean, and Lily's family.
ISBN-13: 978-0-7787-1024-0 (rlb) -- ISBN-10: 0-7787-1024-6 (rlb)
ISBN-13: 978-0-7787-1040-0 (pbk) -- ISBN-10: 0-7787-1040-8 (pbk)
[1. Schools--Fiction.] I. Monks, Lydia, ill. II. Title. III. Series.
PZ7.A263Sh 2005
[E]--dc22
2005001573 LC

Published by Crabtree Publishing in 2005
First published in 2004 by Egmont Books Ltd.

Paperback ISBN 0-7787-1040-8
Reinforced Hardcover Binding ISBN 0-7787-1024-6

1 2 3 4 5 6 7 8 9 0 Printed in Italy 4 3 2 1 0 9 8 7 6 5

Daisy

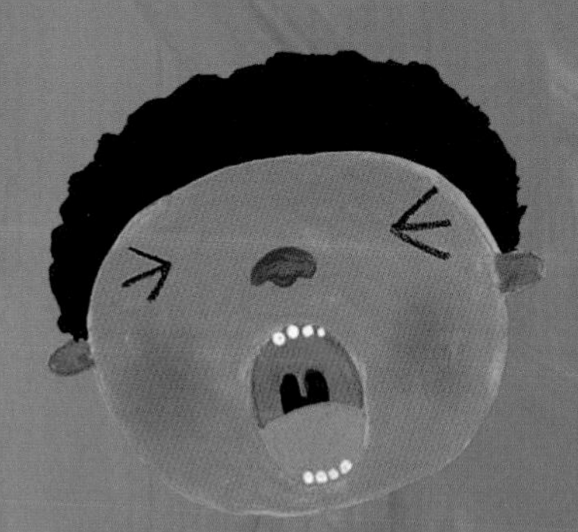

Sean

Lily

For Alice and her friends at

Bounds Green School

K.A.

Daisy

Please, please!

On Monday Mrs. Green asked the class to talk about their weekends.

Daisy put up her hand. But Mrs. Green chose Sean and Amber and Jack.

Daisy bit into her apple with a very loud crunch. Her tooth felt strange.

On Tuesday it was P.E. Daisy didn't want to jump up high in case her tooth wobbled even more.

On Wednesday Lee pointed to the letters while they sang the alphabet song.

Daisy sang very quietly because of her tooth.

On Thursday Daisy really wanted to wash up the paint brushes. Mrs. Green said it was Joe's turn.

On Friday Mrs. Green's class had show and tell while they ate their fruit.

Daisy had forgotten to bring something from home. She felt angry and fed up.

Mrs. Green gave her an apple.

“Here,” she said, “have a bite.”

Daisy had a bite. Her tooth wibbled and wobbled and wibbled some more.

Then it came out, right in the middle of show and tell.

Daisy put up her hand.

“Please, Mrs. Green,” she said. “I

have something I’d like to show.”

And Mrs. Green chose Daisy first of all.

Sean

Jack and Daniel were playing in the jungle. Sean ran in with his dinosaurs. They made a big roaring noise.

"Sean," said Mrs. Green. "Please play quietly."

Sean went to see Amber and Dotun in the home corner. He woke up the baby and the dress-up clothes got messy.

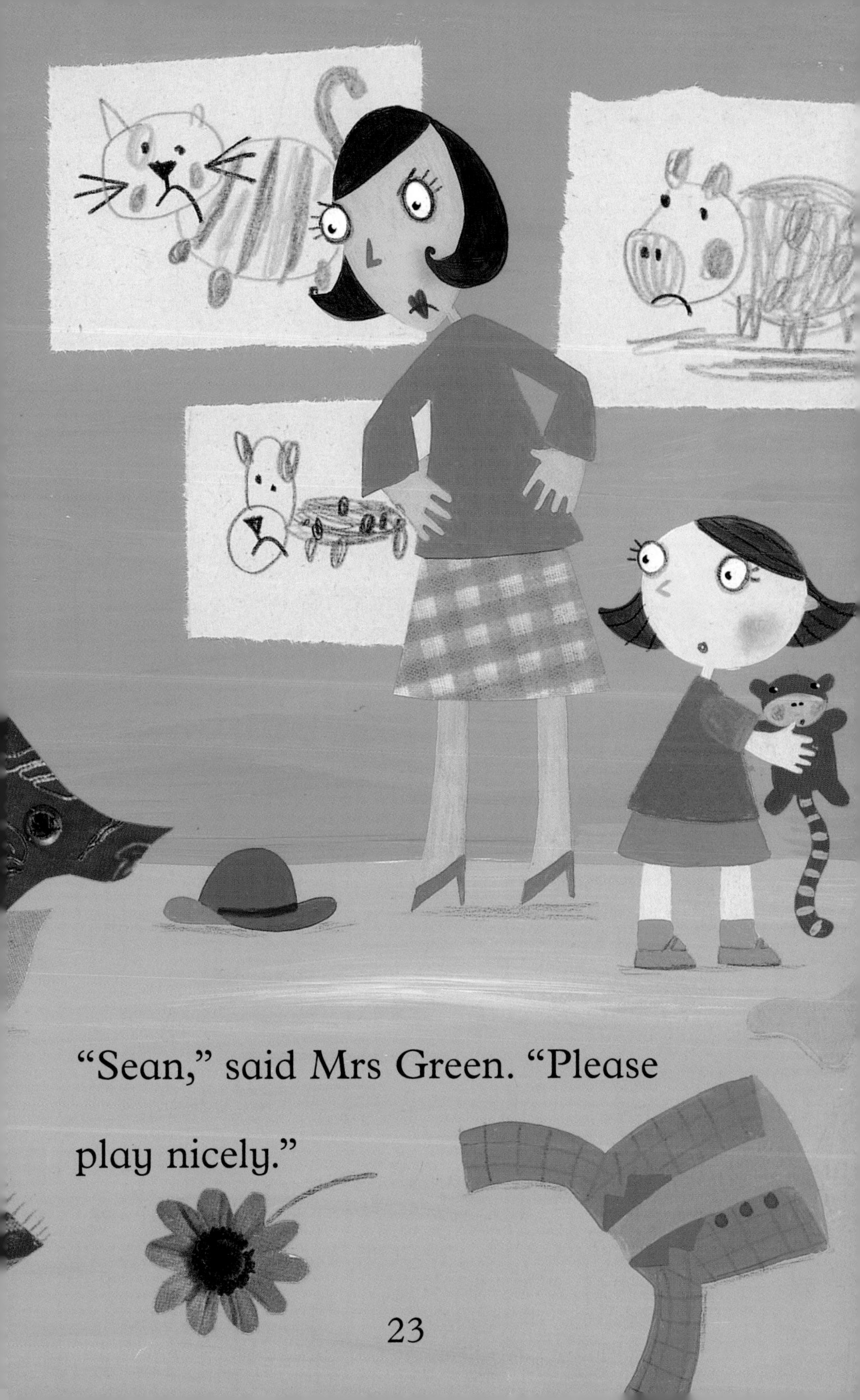

“Sean,” said Mrs Green. “Please play nicely.”

Emma was making bubbles in the water tank. Sean thought a volcano would be much more fun. He put some red paint in the bottle.

"Sean," said Mrs. Green. "You will have to stay in at playtime to tidy up."

Sean put the paints in the corner of the closet.

Mrs. Green came to see.

"Very good," she said. "You can go out to play now."

But the closet door was stuck. Sean was stuck inside. Mrs. Green was stuck too.

“Sean,” said Mrs. Green. “I think

you should try shouting.”

Sean took a deep breath.

He pretended to be a lion and

roared as loud as he could.

ROAR!

Miss Wood came and opened the door with a screwdriver.

"Oh my goodness," she said.

"Were you scared?"

"No," said Mrs. Green. "Not with

Sean here to shout for help."

Lily

Lovely, Joe!

Mrs. Green's class was making books.

They had to draw their homes and

the people who lived there.

Daisy drew her mom and dad and

her brother and her new baby sister.

Dotun drew his mom and dad and his brothers. Then he drew his aunt and cousins, who sometimes came to stay with him.

Jack drew his mom and his dad and his cat and his dog and his fish and his babysitter.

Lily drew her mom and their apartment with a big bowl of flowers. She felt a bit sad.

"Oh dear, Lily," said Mrs. Green.

"You haven't got very far, have you?"

Lily started to cry.

Mrs. Green had an idea. She gave Lily a hug and a new piece of paper. Then she whispered in Lily's ear.

At playtime Lily was still busy drawing and cutting. But when showing time came she was ready.

Lily opened her book very carefully.

Now everybody could see all her houses

and all the people who lived there.

Dad's house had a new bed. Grandma's house had a swing in the garden. Aunt Mary's apartment was a bit messy, but Mom still had her flowers.

And Lily was in all of the pictures.